LIGHT
and
Color

FOR CAROL . . . FOREVER

LIGHT
and Color

By Lawrence F. Lowery

Illustrated by Muriel Wood

National Science Teachers Association
Arlington, Virginia

National Science Teachers Association

Claire Reinburg, Director
Wendy Rubin, Managing Editor
Andrew Cooke, Senior Editor
Amanda O'Brien, Associate Editor
Amy America, Book Acquisitions Coordinator

ART AND DESIGN
Will Thomas Jr., Director
Joseph Butera, Cover, Interior Design
Original illustrations by Muriel Wood

PRINTING AND PRODUCTION
Catherine Lorrain, Director

NATIONAL SCIENCE TEACHERS ASSOCIATION
David L. Evans, Executive Director
David Beacom, Publisher

1840 Wilson Blvd., Arlington, VA 22201
www.nsta.org/store
For customer service inquiries, please call 800-277-5300.

Lexile® measure: 590L

Library of Congress Cataloging-in-Publication Data

Lowery, Lawrence F., author.
  Light and color / Lawrence F. Lowery ; illustrated by Muriel Wood.
      pages cm -- (I wonder why)
  Audience: K to 3.
  ISBN 978-1-938946-51-6 -- ISBN 978-1-938946-52-3 (e-book)
  1. Light--Juvenile literature. 2. Color--Juvenile literature. I. Wood, Muriel, illustrator. II. Title.
  QC360.L695 2014
  535--dc23
                    2014019381

Cataloging-in-Publication Data are also available from the Library of Congress for the e-book.

Introduction

The *I Wonder Why* series is a set of science books created specifically for young learners who are in their first years of school. The content for each book was chosen to be appropriate for youngsters who are beginning to construct knowledge of the world around them. These youngsters ask questions. They want to know about things. They are more curious than they will be when they are a decade older. Research shows that science is students' favorite subject when they enter school for the first time.

Science is both *what* we know and *how* we come to know it. What we know is the content knowledge that accumulates over time as scientists continue to explore the universe in which we live. How we come to know science is the set of thinking and reasoning processes we use to get answers to the questions and inquiries in which we are engaged.

Scientists learn by observing, comparing, and organizing the objects and ideas they are investigating. Children learn the same way. The thinking processes are among several inquiry behaviors that enable us to find out about our world and how it works. Observing, comparing, and organizing are fundamental to the more advanced thinking processes of relating, experimenting, and inferring.

The five books in this set of the *I Wonder Why* series focus on some content of the physical sciences. The physical sciences consist of studies of the physical properties and interactions of energy and inanimate objects as opposed to the study of the characteristics of living things.

Physics, along with mathematics and chemistry, is one of the fundamental sciences because the other sciences, such as botany and zoology, deal with systems that seem to obey the laws of physics. The physical laws of matter, energy, and the fundamental forces of nature govern the interactions between particles and physical entities such as subatomic particles and planets.

These books introduce the reader to several basic physical science ideas: exploration of the properties of some objects (*Rubber vs. Glass*), interaction with the properties of light and the effect of light on objects (*Light and Color; Dark as a Shadow*), the nature of waves and sound (*Sounds Are High, Sounds Are Low*), and the use of simple machines to accomplish work (*Michael's Racing Machine*).

The information in these books leads the characters and the reader to discover how opaque objects block light and cast shadows, that different objects have special and useful properties (glass and rubber), that simple mechanical tools reveal some of the laws of physics, and that "nontouchable items" such as light and sound energy also have distinctive properties.

Each book uses a different approach to take the reader through simple scientific information. One book is expository, providing factual information. Several are narratives that allow a story involving properties of objects and laws of physics to unfold. Another uses poetry to engage the characters in hands-on experiences. The combination of different styles of artwork, different literary ways to present information, and directly observable scientific phenomena brings the content to the reader through several instructional avenues.

In addition, the content in these books supports the criteria set forth by the *Common Core State Standards*. Unlike didactic presentations of knowledge, the content is woven into each book so that its presence is subtle but powerful.

The science activities in the Parent/Teacher Handbook section in each book enable learners to carry out their own investigations related to the content of the book. The materials needed for these activities are easily obtained, and the activities have been tested with youngsters to be sure they are age appropriate.

After completing a science activity, rereading or referring back to the book and talking about connections with the activity can be a deepening experience that stabilizes the learning as a long-term memory.

Our world has many things we like to see—
faces of our parents and friends,
birds flying across the sky,
blooming flowers,
cats and kittens,
dogs and puppies.

All of the things we ever see, we see because of light.
We see things by daylight,
      or by the light of a lamp,
      or by firelight,
      or by flashlight,
      or by moonlight,
      or by some other light.

Outside, on a night when the Moon is not shining,
find a place where it is dark. Look all around.
Can you see anything?

At another time, when you are inside, turn out all the lights.
Then look around. What do you see?

If you see anything, outside or indoors, it is not completely dark.
Without any light, you cannot see anything.

We see because of what light is and what light does.
We don't see light until it hits things such as people and objects.

When light hits something, some of the light bounces away.
Some of that light bounces right into our eyes.

How does light bounce?
You can see how by trying something yourself.
You need a small mirror and a sunny day.

Find a window where sunlight is streaming in.
Hold the mirror so that the sunlight hits it.
Watch for a bright spot of sunlight on the wall.
Move the mirror and watch the spot move.

The sunlight bounces off the mirror
and shines on the wall.

That is one way to see light bounce.

Most of the time we cannot see light bounce. But it bounces anyway. Light has to bounce off an object for us to be able to see that object.

How do we see a painting? Light hits the painting and bounces away. Some of the light bounces back to us. It goes into our eyes, and we see the painting.

How do we see people? Light hits the people, then it bounces away. Some of the light bounces back to us. It goes into our eyes, and we see the people.

We can see people, places, and things
      by daylight,
      by the light of a lamp,
      by firelight,
      and by the light of the Moon.

Light of some kind is needed for us to see.

Look at the brown tree trunk in
this picture.
How can it be brown? Brown is not
a rainbow color.

Scientists have found that the colors you see that are not in the rainbow are
mixtures of the rainbow colors.

When red and green light are mixed, they make the color yellow.

When green and blue mix, they make a color called cyan.

When blue and red mix, they make the color magenta.

And do you remember what color is made when all the colors are mixed together?

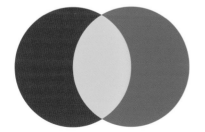
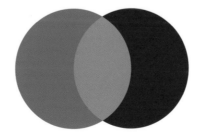

Look at the green leaf in the boy's hands in the picture, or look at a real leaf that is green.

When light falls on the leaf, all the colors in light soak into the leaf, except the color green. The green part of light bounces back into your eyes, and you see a green leaf.

Take a look at some other things.

A red rose soaks up every color in light but red. The red part of light bounces back to you.

A lemon soaks up every color in light but yellow. The lemon bounces the yellow light back to you.

If you see the color blue, it is because the blue part of light is bouncing back into your eyes.

You might wonder why you see things in different colors.

All light is made up of rainbow colors. When the rainbow colors are mixed together, they give us white light.

You can make a rainbow if you can get
a piece of glass shaped like the one in
the picture. A piece of glass like this is
called a prism.

When light passes through the glass prism,
a wonderful thing happens.

The light, which you cannot see, breaks apart
in the glass and makes a rainbow.

Light is made up of all the colors in a rainbow.
When those colors are together, we see the color white.

Every color we see comes from light.
When those colors come out of light, we see a rainbow.

The colors of a rainbow are the colors in light:
red,
orange,
yellow,
green,
blue,
violet.

We see because of light
and because of the wonderful way our eyes are made.

We see things in color.
Color is another wonderful thing about light.

All the colors we see come from light.
Without light, we would not see colors.

Light is very important.

Light enables us to see.

The way light bounces off everything into our eyes
gives us information about our world.

The light from a fire may be dim or bright.
It is never as bright as the light from the Sun.
But like the Sun, firelight enables me to see you.

The light from a flashlight or the Moon at night
is very much the same. And like the Sun, those lights
enable you to see me, too.

What else gives off light?
Fireflies do,
fireworks,
and lightning, too.

In the dark of night, the light from an
electric lamp helps you see.

Where does light come from?

Daylight is sunlight. That light comes from the Sun.

All day long, light from the Sun enables you to see.

All objects in our world are seen by our eyes as a result of light waves reflecting from the object and entering our eyes. If no light waves reflect from the object, it appears black to the human eye. If all wavelengths (all colors of light) reflect from the object, it appears white. Thus, the surface structures of various objects both absorb and reflect various colors of light. A green leaf appears green because its surface absorbs all the colors of the light spectrum except green, which is reflected.

Besides reflection of light from the surface of materials, this book introduces the idea of diffraction of light. Diffraction is the separation of the various wavelengths of light into colors as it passes through a material. A glass prism diffracts light waves to produce the spectrum of colors from white light—red, orange, yellow, green, blue, and violet.

THE PRIMARY COLORS OF LIGHT

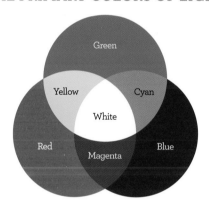

THE PRIMARY COLORS OF PIGMENTS

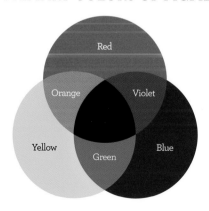

NOTE: The mixing of light colors produces colors that are different than the mixing of paint or dyes.

Science Activities

Observing That White Light Can Be Separated Into Colors

Sunlight is made up of all the colors of the rainbow. The colors appear in the same order when separated: red, orange, yellow, green, blue, and violet. You can separate the colors that make up white light in a darkened room, preferably one with white walls or ceiling. Lean a small mirror in a full, clear glass of water. Shine a bright beam of light through the water at the mirror. Adjust the mirror so that the light reflects from the mirror to the ceiling or a wall. The beam of light through the water will separate the colors in the light and reflect them off the mirror to the wall. What colors do you see? When the white sunlight travels through the water, it produces a rainbow. What colors do you see in a rainbow?

Jiggle the water in the glass. What do you see on the wall or ceiling? Do the colors mix again and make a spot of white on the wall or ceiling?

If you can obtain a prism, hold it in direct sunlight or in front of a bright beam of light. Slowly rotate the prism until a spectrum of colors appears on a wall or ceiling. The sunlight passes through the glass and separates the light into a rainbow of colors.

Rainbows in the sky appear when sunlight passes through raindrops in the air.

Additional activities can be found at www.nsta.org/light.

Parent/Teacher Handbook

Introduction

Light and Color is a child's introduction to light and its relationship to the color of objects. This book for young children lays a foundation for science concepts students will learn in middle school that are only possible with early learning experiences.

Inquiry Processes

All of the knowledge that we acquire comes to us through our five senses. Our sense of sight provides us with all the visual images we store in our brains; thus, the process of using our eyes to observe is very important to our understanding of the world around us. This book focuses on the scientific processes of observing and comparing observations to understand a property of light and its importance to what we see. By stressing the sense of sight, young readers will realize the importance of using this sense to learn about the phenomenon we call light.

Content

Light is a form of energy. The visible spectrum or band of colors known as light appears white when all the wavelengths of the colors are mixed together. Light is part of the larger group or band of energy waves known as the electromagnetic spectrum. Other examples in the electromagnetic spectrum are radio waves, infrared rays, ultraviolet rays, and x-rays.

One of the main differences between one colored light and another is the wavelength. *Wavelength* refers to the distance between waves or pulses of light energy. Each color in the visual spectrum has its own wavelength.

White light is a mixture of the colors we see in a rainbow. White light is the combining of all of the color wavelengths. When light hits an object, some of the colors (wavelengths) can be taken into the object (absorbed) and some can be bounced back (reflected). If the object reflects all the colors, the object looks white like this page. If the object looks black, the object absorbs all the light and looks like the ink on this page. No colors bounce back.

THE ELECTROMAGNETIC SPECTRUM

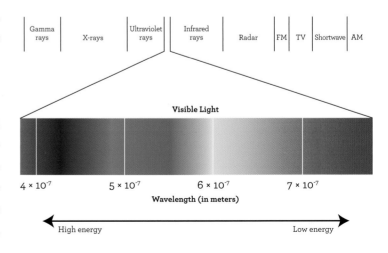